BATMAN & ROBIN
ADVENTURES

POISON IVY'S
RAINFOREST REVENGE

BY SARAH HINES STEPHENS

ILLUSTRATED BY
TIM LEVINS

COVER ILLUSTRATION BY
LUCIANO VECCHIO

CONTENTS

CHAPTER 1

CLEAR AS DAY

At twilight, a long line of cars began to arrive at Gotham City Conservatory. Limousines and expensive cars delivered well-dressed guests to the front of the glittering glass building.

The conservatory had been closed to the public for several months for major restorations. Now everyone was excited to go inside the newly remodelled building to see the display of plants presented by the Conservatory Campaign.

Bruce Wayne's black car was the last in line. As the billionaire businessman climbed out, no one suspected that the Dark Knight – Batman – was actually in their midst! Safe in his secret identity, Bruce paused, took a deep breath and admired the building. The restoration had been a success.

Bruce looked towards Robinson Park, one of the city's largest green spaces. The park was next to the freshly refurbished conservatory and stood in stark contrast. For years, Robinson Park had been neglected and poorly maintained. Paths and bridges were in disrepair. Litter was strewn everywhere, and the plants that had managed to grow needed pruning. But all of that was about to change.

Tonight's event was a fundraiser by the Conservatory Campaign to benefit Robinson Park. Bruce hoped it would raise enough money to return the park to its former glory.

Tim Drake – the secret identity of Batman's crime-fighting partner, Robin – climbed out of the car next. Disguised as Bruce Wayne's ward, he was also smartly dressed for this formal event. But Tim was in a much bigger hurry to get inside. He gazed up at the elegant building. Three storeys of glass, framed in white, glowed in the twilight.

"WHOOOO!" Tim let out a low whistle.

The conservatory looked like something out of a fairy tale! The display inside the huge greenhouse was sure to be just as wonderful.

Tim cleared his throat to let Bruce know he was ready to go in.

"Sorry, Tim." Bruce smiled at the boy and placed a hand on his shoulder. "I thought I could smell something."

At the end of a red carpet, waiters carrying trays of glasses and appetizers welcomed the pair through double doors. Inside the conservatory the air was warm and damp – perfect for growing plants. A fountain burbled in the corner while the city's richest patrons nibbled and sipped.

"Mr Wayne!" Tim's chaperone was immediately surrounded by guests. His wealth and power rarely went unnoticed. Everyone wanted his attention. If they only knew his true identity!

Luckily, Tim did not draw as much attention. Nobody noticed as the teenage boy slipped away from the crowd to take a look at what he had really come to see.

All around the room rare plants were on display. The unusual specimens had been collected from rainforests all over the world.

Tim found them fascinating and slowly studied each one. Some varieties had extraordinary adaptations and many were carnivorous!

The nepenthes captured his attention first. These meat-eating flowers looked like rearing snakes with deep cup-like hollows. When an insect or small mammal fell inside the hollow, it would be caught in sticky liquid. While trapped at the bottom of the large open chamber, it would slowly be digested.

Beside the nepenthes were large Venus flytraps. The flytraps had hinged 'jaws' made up of two leaf-like structures that snapped shut on flying insects. And next to the flytraps were more insect-eating plants that grew sweet-smelling sticky paths to lead insects to their doom.

As Tim walked over to look at a display of rare vines, he noticed that most of the party guests were clustered in one area. They were flocked around a beautiful raven-haired woman dressed all in emerald green who seemed to have captured everyone's attention. Even Bruce Wayne's.

But the plants were what had captured Tim's imagination. As he approached the next exhibit, Tim thought he saw one of the enormous ferns unfurl before his eyes. It looked like it was reaching out to touch the guests. Beside it, another plant also appeared to be moving!

Tim rubbed his eyes and looked again. He scanned the room to see if anyone else could see what he was seeing. But everyone in the crowd was staring intently at the dark-haired woman in green.

The woman was telling them about one of her favourite flowers. She held a special variety in her hand. She moved it slowly past each of the admiring faces in the crowd, so everyone could take a close look.

"Mmm . . . isn't the scent divine?" she asked. She breathed in deeply, encouraging her captive audience to do the same. Then she let her breath out with a sigh and a mysterious smile.

Tim wondered briefly who the woman could be. Her long, black hair cascaded over half of her face, making it difficult to see her eyes. Could she be the botanist in charge? He didn't have much time to ponder before something else caught his eye.

Above the gathered guests he spied more moving plants! Several hanging shrubs appeared to be sending down sticky tendrils.

Pushing past a man in a dark suit, Tim tried to take a closer look. But the people were packed in too closely. Nobody would budge. Nobody wanted to step away from the woman and her captivating flower.

Tim ducked behind a guest in a red gown, trying to spot Bruce Wayne in the crowd. Something felt wrong, and he didn't like it. The harder he tried to get to Bruce the more the crowd seemed to push in tighter. Tim could not get through.

"I give up," Tim said to himself. But then he had a brilliant idea.

Tim stepped outside and took a deep breath of the cool, clear air. He turned around to look at the building he'd just left. Although the glass was a bit fogged, Tim had a better view of what was happening in the greenhouse from the outside.

And what he saw was shocking!

Tim had been right about the plants. They *were* moving. In fact, they were making a move! The fern frond he'd seen uncurling earlier was now stretching towards a short man's suit pocket. The long tendrils dropping down from the hanging baskets were winding themselves onto expensive necklaces and other jewels. Not only that, they were unclasping them!

While Tim looked on, the plants withdrew, taking wallets and jewellery with them. The plants were pickpocketing!

Tim knocked loudly on the glass walls to alert Gotham City's wealthiest citizens that they were being robbed. He yelled and pointed frantically, but nobody paid any attention. It was as if the guests were all in some sort of trance.

Tim pounded again, searching the crowd, trying to find Bruce Wayne. Surely Batman's alter ego had noticed what was going on. At last Tim spotted his companion. He was standing right beside the lady in green. Tim spotted something else, too . . .

The woman in the emerald dress was the only one still wearing any jewellery. A slim gold bracelet was wound around her delicate wrist. The three-leaf design of the bangle reminded Tim of something . . .

Before Tim could put the clues together the woman reached up and removed the long black wig she'd been wearing. A mane of long red locks cascaded down and over her shoulders.

Tim sucked in his breath. He was looking at Gotham City's very own vining villain, Poison Ivy!

Cursing himself for not working it out sooner, Tim put the pieces of the evening together in his head, puzzling out the devious plot. Poison Ivy must have gassed everyone in the conservatory with toxic spores released from inside the flower she was so anxious to share. Once the guests were in a stupor, Poison Ivy and her plant assistants had robbed them of their valuables!

The leafy thief had almost got away with her crime too. But she had not counted on one thing – a pair of uninvited guests.

CHAPTER 2

FLOWER POWER

Behind the great glass building, Tim found Bruce Wayne's car and the outfit he had hidden inside. It took only a moment for the dressed-up teen to transform into Robin, Boy Wonder!

After getting rid of his black suit, Robin raced back to the conservatory. He didn't have to worry about being seen through the glass walls, because the guests inside were staggering around in a haze. All but one.

Poison Ivy was stroking the leaf of one of her plant helpers as though it was a pet. Clearly she was safe from the spores she'd unleashed on the rest of the crowd. But Bruce Wayne was not. Batman's alter ego looked dazed. Robin had to get to him – and fast!

Using his grapnel and a rope, Robin climbed to the top of the tall building without any trouble. He balanced on the glass dome and took a rebreather mask from his Utility Belt. He couldn't risk breathing in any of Poison Ivy's toxic spores. When the mask was secure, Robin dropped down through the greenhouse vent.

FWHIPP!

Robin landed right behind Poison Ivy. He could have grabbed the botanical burglar easily, but there was something else he had to do first.

Running at full speed Robin tackled Bruce Wayne.

OOOF!

He rolled with the him right out of the front door.

"You need some air," Robin told the billionaire gravely. Bruce nodded groggily, but did not speak. Robin could see he was trying to gather his strength.

Robin helped Bruce sit up and lean against a wall. Then the Boy Wonder raced back inside. He didn't have time to wait for his partner to recover fully. He just had to hope that he would.

Inside the plant palace things had gone from bad to worse. The guests were no longer dazed and staggering. They were actually wilting!

Many of the guests were falling to their knees, slouching over in their chairs and putting their heads down on tables. Those still standing looked as green as Poison Ivy's emerald-coloured evening dress.

Then a green flash caught Robin's eye. Poison Ivy was fleeing into another room. He had to get to her before she got away!

Scanning the conservatory's lush interior, Robin spotted something that might help. A long creeping vine was hanging from the overhead display. It looked sturdy and thick – thick enough to hold the weight of a teenage boy!

Robin took three running steps, leaped and reached out for the living rope. He caught the vine with both hands.

FWOOHM!

Robin sailed over the collapsing guests towards Poison Ivy. The green villain whirled and saw the Boy Wonder zooming through the air.

In an instant, the vine Robin was holding sprouted thorns! Large, nasty spikes sliced through his gloves and dug into his palms. He let go and fell.

CRASH!

The young hero landed on the buffet table. Food and dishes flew into the air before splattering and shattering on the floor. Robin slid off the table and clattered to the ground along with them.

By the time Robin struggled back up to his feet, Poison Ivy was even closer to the rear exit. Grabbing an unbroken plate, Robin flung it as hard as he could.

The plate spun like a flying saucer. It hit the wall next to Poison Ivy, shattering one of the panes of glass that made up the conservatory walls. Robin picked up another plate and another.

FWHIP! SMASH! FWHIP! SMASH!

With each throw he got closer to his fleeing target.

But with each throw Poison Ivy got closer to the exit!

"Hold it right there!" a voice shouted from above them.

Batman dropped down from the ceiling – right into Robin's line of fire!

The Dark Knight's cape swirled around him. He grabbed a plate out of the air with one hand, a split-second before it struck his breastplate.

With his other hand, Batman grabbed Poison Ivy's wrist. She dropped her bag of stolen goods and staggered back, wrenching her hand from his grasp.

"You!" Poison Ivy spat. Her eyes narrowed as she glared at the Caped Crusader.

"Have you missed me, Ivy?" Batman growled back.

"Not as much as you're going to miss me!" Ivy replied. She whirled and started running back towards the exit.

Batman was not about to let her get away. He seized a Batarang from his Utility Belt and threw it at Poison Ivy. The weighted rope attached to the bat-shaped weapon coiled around her ankles, binding her legs together.

Ivy fell and hit the floor hard.

OOOF!

Batman swooped past her, blocking the exit. Robin moved in from the other side. They had her surrounded!

But Poison Ivy was not done. She shot a hand into the air and summoned a vine – the same one Robin had tried to use earlier – but now the thorns were gone.

Ivy let the vine pull her to her feet. Then a slow smile bloomed on her face.

"What are you going to do now, Bats?" she asked in a teasing voice. Still clinging to her vine she motioned around the great glass hall.

Guests everywhere were gasping for air. They sprawled on the ground and slumped over tables, chairs and plants. They needed to get out of the toxin-filled building as soon as possible!

Poison Ivy laughed as her vine lifted her up and away. She knew Batman would not come after her when there were so many innocent people to save.

The Dark Knight had no choice. He let Ivy go and kneeled down to pick up the person closest to him. He threw the gasping man over his shoulder. He tucked a second guest under his arm and raced for the exit. Robin followed his partner's lead. Without so much as a backward glance towards the retreating villain, he pulled a woman onto his back and ran for safety.

The Dynamic Duo carried guest after guest out of the deadly environment. They placed the well-dressed men and women on the grass in the cool night air. Slowly Gotham City's elite began to come around, coughing and sitting up.

WEEOO WEEOO WEEOO

Robin heard sirens approaching. Batman had used the radio in his cowl to summon emergency services. Within moments they had arrived and were checking on the guests.

Robin lingered, helping the workers with the recovering guests. But soon he noticed that Batman was not there. Robin found his partner standing in the shadows nearby. The Dark Knight was deep in thought. Or perhaps he was worried.

"Don't worry. They're going to be fine," Robin reported, waving an arm towards the guests.

Batman nodded, grimly. He knew all too well about the many lethal toxins and spores in Poison Ivy's arsenal. He was glad to hear the guests would be all right.

But Ivy herself had slipped away. And Batman had a feeling that this trouble was far from over. In fact, he suspected it was just beginning . . .

***

The next morning Tim woke up early, as he did most days at Wayne Manor. He padded downstairs for breakfast, only to meet Alfred, Bruce Wayne's butler, who was standing at the foot of the stairs.

Alfred greeted Tim warmly and escorted him into the adjoining study. Master Wayne was sitting in the quiet room reading the morning newspaper.

Two cups of tea sat steaming on a side table. Alfred had been expecting the boy.

"Good morning," Bruce said without lowering his paper. "Have a seat."

Tim returned the greeting but could not bring himself to sit down. Instead he paced back and forth in front of the table that ran along the windows while he waited for his mentor to finish reading.

Since the attack at the conservatory, Tim had been irritated. Batman had mentioned that he thought Ivy's dangerous trick was probably just the beginning of a bigger plot. And Tim could not stop wondering what else the menace might have up her green sleeves. To make matters worse, nobody had seen her since the incident. The whole situation was making Tim feel . . . itchy.

Sunlight streamed in from the outside, lighting up a row of tiny potted trees displayed on a large table inside the study. Alfred bent over one of the miniature trees with a tiny pair of pruning shears.

SNIP! SNIP!

The butler used the delicate tool to trim and shape a small Cypress. The tiny tree looked just like a full-size windswept evergreen in miniature.

Tim paused. He hadn't ever really looked at Bruce's bonsai tree collection before. But he was too upset to admire it for long.

"What I don't understand is why Poison Ivy would attack the conservatory," Tim finally blurted, interrupting his mentor's reading. "Doesn't she *like* plants?"

Bruce's paper rustled. Slowly he lowered it and picked up his tea. "I'd say that's putting it mildly," he said, taking a sip. "The criminal we're chasing was once just a shy girl who was led astray by the evil botanist, Dr Woodrue. He replaced Ivy's blood with chlorophyll."

"The green stuff in plants?" Tim asked.

"Yes," Bruce nodded. "But that wasn't all. He also injected her with a whole host of allergens. She's filled with toxins and is truly part plant herself. She doesn't just like plants, Tim. She identifies with them."

"And controls them," Alfred added.

"So, wouldn't she like a place that's built especially *for* plants?" Tim asked. "Like the conservatory?"

To Tim, conservatories seemed like safe havens for plants that needed extra moisture and protection from nature's harshest elements. Indoors the tender leaves and shoots and flowers were safe from too much heat or cold or wind.

"Why would she steal from people who are supporting a plant *palace*?" Tim asked.

Bruce took another sip of tea and folded up his newspaper.

"Perhaps, to Ivy, the conservatory seems more like a plant prison," Bruce mused. "But I still feel like there is more to it than just stealing from the guests who were attending the benefit. The conservatory restoration was already completed. All of the money donated that evening was intended to pay for the restoration of Robinson Park."

Bruce stood and walked over to the bonsai table. He paused before a tiny maple tree with miniature leaves that were beginning to turn bright colours.

"You know, Tim, bonsai trees grow old but remain small because we trim them and keep them in small containers. To many, bonsai is an art form, but to Poison Ivy it might seem like . . ." Bruce trailed off.

"But, Master Wayne, if we didn't trim the trees they would grow far too large to keep indoors," Alfred pointed out. "Sometimes a little pruning is necessary, to keep things in order, so that everyone can enjoy them. And so that we can all live together."

Tim could see Alfred's point, but he wondered how Poison Ivy would feel about that. She probably didn't think plants should be walled or trimmed or tamed or controlled at all! She probably wanted everything to grow wild.

Bruce turned and walked back to his newspaper. He looked again at the headline: WORK TO BEGIN AT ROBINSON PARK. Then he looked up, straight at Tim.

"I think I know where Poison Ivy is hiding," Bruce said.

CHAPTER 3
PUTTING DOWN ROOTS

Bruce and Tim disappeared into the Batcave without finishing their tea. A few moments later, dressed as Batman and Robin, they jumped into the Batmobile. The Dark Knight fired up the engine and zoomed out of the Batcave!

"I don't know why I didn't think of it before," Batman said. He hugged the turns as he sped towards Robinson Park.

Poison Ivy had made the city green space her lair once before. Batman felt sure she had taken over the space again. He was also pretty sure he knew why.

The Batmobile came to stop beside a large roadblock. The street that passed through the park was closed to traffic so that workers could bring in the trucks and equipment they would need for the park reconstruction. Though, from the look of things, they hadn't been able to get very far.

A small fleet of excavators and other equipment stood at the ready. Before them stood a dense green wall of foliage. The park was so overgrown it looked like a jungle!

"I knew the park needed a lot of work, but this . . ." Robin trailed off.

"This is not normal," Batman reassured the Boy Wonder.

The Dark Knight stepped out of the Batmobile and walked closer to the heavy machinery. Workers were standing around looking at the equipment. Some were even scratching their heads.

"Let's go!" the crew boss shouted. But nothing happened.

In the bulldozer closest to Batman and Robin, the driver turned her key. The bulldozer made a grinding noise.

POW! BANG! PUH!

The bulldozer popped and banged. Then the machine coughed out a puff of dark smoke and was silent.

Beside the bulldozer, a backhoe operator couldn't even get to his seat! The enormous machine was so covered in overgrowth it looked like it was being eaten by the jungle.

The backhoe operator hacked away the vines entangling his vehicle, but they grew back as quickly as he could tear them away. Finally the operator gave up in frustration and stormed away.

Batman strode slowly over to the large dumper truck that was next in the queue. The vehicle's driver looked puzzled as he stared into the fuel tank.

"We filled up every vehicle in the fleet yesterday so we would be ready to work today. But now I can't get the truck to start at all!" he explained.

The truck driver grabbed a torch from his cab and directed the beam of light into the dark fuel tank. Batman leaned in for a closer look. Then he and the driver both stepped back in surprise. The tank had a huge colony of mushrooms growing inside it!

"What in the world?" the driver gasped. He didn't understand why or how fungus was budding in the fuel tank of his truck. But the Dark Knight had a pretty good idea how it had happened and who was behind the mischief.

This mushroom mayhem was the work of one woman: Poison Ivy.

"Your equipment's been sabotaged," Batman told the crew boss. "Somewhere in that overgrowth is someone who does not want you working in the park."

"It looks like you were right about where Poison Ivy is hiding," Robin said, angling his head towards the wriggling plants taking over Robinson Park.

"But how in the world are we going to get in there?" Robin asked.

The Boy Wonder could barely take his eyes off of the teeming jungle. It was writhing and growing larger and more tangled with each passing moment. It looked completely impassable. But Batman knew there had to be a way inside.

"Let's take it from the top!" said the Caped Crusader.

Firing his grapnel, Batman snared one of the tallest plants in the jungle canopy. The line recoiled, and the Dark Knight was hauled up to the highest point on the great green mass. Soon Robin was at his side.

The view from their new perch did not give Robin much hope. From the top, the dense jungle looked even thicker, and it stretched as far as the eye could see.

"I still don't see how we're going to get to the bottom of this." Robin shook his head.

Batman looked thoughtfully at the tangled growth. "We're going to be like rain," Batman explained. No matter how thickly plants grew, it was essential that rain could make its way to their roots. Batman had a plan to travel into the overgrowth like a large water droplet.

The Dark Knight stepped further into the canopy. He spied an extra large vine, twisting up from below.

SWOOOOOSH!

He leaped onto it and rode it like a twisted slide. He dropped down underneath the leaf layer and kept going.

Robin took the same path, and the pair slid deeper into the jungle. When the vine grew too tangled the duo leaped from giant leaf to giant leaf, using the huge plants like a living staircase.

They were nearing the forest floor when Robin stepped onto the edge of an enormous flower. The centre of the bloom opened like a yawning mouth. The surface of the blossom was covered in a slippery liquid, and Robin lost his footing as soon as he hit the shiny surface. He tried to step back to steady himself, but he'd been moving too fast! His feet went out from under him, and he slid into the cavernous blossom.

SPLASH!

Robin landed at the bottom of the giant liquid-filled flower. He was trapped like a helpless insect.

Robin scrambled to get to the side of the deep pool. He tried to stay calm, but he realized he had fallen into a super-sized version of the nepenthe plants he'd seen at the conservatory.

The Boy Wonder knew all too well that the liquid in the mouth of the flower wasn't water – it was a digestive enzyme. If he didn't get out of the trap soon, he would be eaten alive!

Robin swam to the side and reached up. The walls of the plant were too slick to climb. There was nothing to hold onto and nowhere to put his feet. Treading liquid, he fired his grapnel towards the mouth of the flower. But the metal hook bounced off the thick petal wall. There was no way out!

"Robin!" Batman's voice echoed in the floral chamber. "Swim towards the bottom of the flower!"

Robin could not believe what he was hearing. Batman wanted him to plunge completely into the lethal liquid he was trying to get out of?

"There's no way to climb out," Batman shouted. "Swim down. I'll meet you at the base."

Robin grabbed the rebreather from his Utility Belt. He took a deep breath and positioned it in his mouth. Then, summoning all of his courage and will, he dived down into the goo. Robin trusted his partner. Batman always had a plan.

Robin kicked hard towards the bottom. It was dark inside the flower, and the pool felt like it had no end. But Robin kept kicking until he finally felt something solid under his hands. He had reached the bottom of the enormous blossom.

The base of the flower felt smooth. He felt all around but could not find any edges or holes or ways out. The flower's liquid began to sting Robin's exposed skin.

Robin felt the walls more frantically. Perhaps Batman had been wrong. Perhaps there was no way out. It was a thought Robin could not allow himself to think!

At last Robin felt a vibration through the flower wall. Then he saw a tiny ray of light. Batman was slicing through the thick plant with the toothed edge of a Batarang. He sawed quickly. As soon as there was a breech in the petal wall, the sticky liquid in the plant began gushing out.

WOOSH!

And with it came Robin.

Batman quickly sprayed down his partner with a pressurized water canister he kept on his Utility Belt. The shower stopped the digestive juices from dissolving Robin's clothes and burning his skin.

"Thanks," Robin said, dripping in the dense undergrowth.

Batman put a hand on the boy's shoulder. He was glad his young partner was safe.

"Obviously Poison Ivy has increased the growth of these plants, and she seems to have increased their deadlier aspects as well," Batman cautioned his friend. "We need to stay alert."

Robin could only nod. He knew the Dark Knight was right, and he felt foolish for getting caught in a trap intended for insects!

The crime fighters slowed their pace as they continued to pick their way through the web of plants. The going was tough and time-consuming. Robin wasn't sure how they would ever find Poison Ivy in the knotted jungle maze.

Batman considered each step carefully before moving forwards. He knew that one false move could lead to disaster.

Still, he wondered if there might be a quicker method to draw Poison Ivy away from this, her preferred environment. His mind wandered, searching for a solution. There had to be another way . . .

The brief moment of distraction was all that it took.

The Caped Crusader placed his boot on a leaf nearly as large as he was. The huge leaf had thin, red spines that extended around all of its edges. The instant his foot touched the surface, it quivered and sent a shiver up its stem. Then a second spined leaf clamped down on Batman from above.

SNAP!

The two leaves closed around him like a giant jaw.

AHHH!

It happened so fast that all Robin heard was a muffled shout. And all he saw was a corner of his partner's cape sticking out of the sealed plant.

"Batman!" Robin yelled and darted towards him.

Another mistake.

Robin's quick motion attracted a number of strangling vines. The sinewy creepers dropped down from branches above like a family of jungle snakes. Before he even knew what they were doing, the vines wound themselves tightly around the young hero's arms and legs.

Robin was trapped as well!

Robin fought against the vines, but the more he struggled the tighter the vines grew. They cut painfully into his wrists and ankles.

"Hold still, Robin!" Batman shouted. He had managed to free his head, but his arms and legs and all of the tools on his Utility Belt were still sealed tightly in the man-eating plant.

"I . . . can't . . . move . . ." Wrapped in living ropes, Robin could not help his partner. He could not even help himself.

The Dynamic Duo was trapped.

CHAPTER 4

QUEEN OF THE JUNGLE

"Well, well, well . . ." Poison Ivy stepped out from behind an enormous fern. Once again she was dressed all in green. But this time she wore her typical one-piece outfit. Matching gloves covered her hands, protecting plants and animals from her toxic touch.

"What have we got here?" she asked. A thin smile played on her red lips. "Unwanted guests that buzz around in my garden are likely to get caught in traps," she teased.

"Who made you queen of this jungle?" Robin shot back. He could only see Poison Ivy out of the corner of his eye. He thrashed this way and that, trying to get a clear view of what the lethal prowler was up to. But the snake-like vines he was trapped in grew tighter each time he moved. The pain was almost unbearable!

"Hello, Poison Ivy," Batman greeted his old enemy calmly. He was almost completely encased in the mouth of an enormous meat-eating plant, but the tone of his voice was totally calm. "Your spores cast quite the spell the other night. You certainly seemed to have an intoxicating effect on Gotham City's elite."

Poison Ivy laughed at the joke. "Ah, yes. Though not toxic enough to befuddle a bat," she added.

Ivy stepped closer to Batman. The flowers and plants around her formed steps. As she walked they wove themselves into positions to support their champion. She stroked the leaves tenderly as she passed. It was clear the jungle was very loyal to her.

Batman couldn't move. He could not reach the weapons and tools he had on his Utility Belt. All he could do was stand there, encased in a deadly plant.

Poison Ivy put her face close to Batman, and he was grateful for the air filters built into his cowl. When she spoke again her tone was harsh.

"What *are* you doing here, anyway?" she demanded.

"Putting a stop to you," Robin shouted back from the spot where he was hanging.

"But you got your jewels. Your rich socialites are safe. You and your people are free to live your lives on your *paved* streets, in your *concrete* buildings, stuck behind *glass*. Why shouldn't my plants and I be afforded the same courtesy? To live how we like? All we want to do is live here, in our tiny green corner . . . wild and free!"

"But this is a city park. It's supposed to be for all of the citizens of Gotham City," the Boy Wonder said.

"No!" Ivy raised her chin in defiance. "Humans and plants cannot live together! Humans are the enemies of plants!"

As Poison Ivy spoke, the plants around her reacted to her anger. Their colours grew a shade darker. Their leaves curled and shrivelled. The vines around Robin dug deeper into his skin.

"Just look at you humans. You're killing rainforests. You're smothering the Earth. You're pulling up native species and enslaving them! Humans have no place here." Poison Ivy was seething.

Robin had to stop himself from laughing out loud. Poison Ivy's view was so limited!

"Humans have been living with plants for as long as there have been humans on the planet," Batman calmly explained. "Not all humans are killing rainforests. We need each other."

Poison Ivy turned back to Batman. She glared at him through narrowed green eyes. "Humans need plants, that's true," she said, thoughtfully. "But plants don't need humans!"

"Ivy, be reasonable." Batman tried to negotiate.

"I am being reasonable," Poison Ivy snarled. "You and your human friends have a big debt to pay the plant world. And I'm going to make sure everyone pays their share. Starting with you."

Batman cocked his head.

Robin looked alarmed.

"That's right, Batman. You're going to feed this lovely dionaea muscipula. You'll make a delightful dinner for her, I'm sure. And you must admit it's a fine last act for a do-gooder like you."

Poison Ivy walked over and ran her hand along the closed flytrap, caressing it. "This lovely specimen will be drawing strength from your remains for a *loooong* time. Of course, that means she will be digesting you for a long time too. You are quite the catch, Batman."

Poison Ivy giggled. Then she spun to face Robin. "And you. You can just hang around here and watch it all happen," she snarled.

"You're going to just leave me here?" Robin asked in disbelief.

"Of course. Enjoy the view for as long as you'd like. When you begin to shrivel and dry out, the vines will release you. They'll drop you onto their roots, so that you can return to the earth . . . as compost."

Robin was speechless. Not even Batman had anything to say.

Satisfied that her work was done, Ivy turned to go. She was immediately lifted up and away by quick-growing vines. A path opened in the dense foliage, like parting curtains, and then immediately closed behind her. Within seconds, all that remained was the echo of her laughter.

"Why, that nasty WEED!" Robin cursed and struggled harder against the vines that held him, making them contract further. Soon his shouts turned into cries of pain.

"Relax, Robin." Batman's voice was calm and soothing.

"How can I relax when we're both trapped and Poison Ivy is getting away?" Robin shouted. His face was red with both effort and anger.

"It's the only way out," Batman said, even more calmly. "Just go limp."

Batman was asking the impossible. But Robin followed his instructions. He took a deep breath and forced himself to stop struggling. He called on his martial arts training to help him clear his mind. He let his body go slack. His pulse slowed.

A minute passed. Then two. And then Robin felt the vines begin to relax too. They loosened their hold.

FWUMPH!

Robin fell onto the jungle floor. He was free of the vines!

He stood up and dusted himself off. "But, why did . . ." Robin stammered.

"When you stopped moving the vines thought you were dead," said Batman. "They released you to be absorbed into the soil and nourish their roots."

Robin shook his head in disbelief. Twice he had almost been eaten by a plant! Robin was free, but his partner was still trapped inside one!

"Hold on, Batman! I'll get you out of there."

Taking his bo staff from his belt, Robin extended it. He tried to insert one end into the flytrap, to pry open the mouth of the plant. Even with leverage, he could not break the seal.

"Try heat," Batman directed.

Robin took several small flash pots from his belt. He ignited them as close to the plant, and as far from Batman's head, as he could get.

Batman's instincts were correct. The plant wilted slightly, shrinking away from the small bursts of flame. The gaps they left in the seal were small, but they were just enough.

Robin dug his bo staff into one of the openings. He pulled down to pry the two leaves apart. He used all of his body weight, and the sticky trap opened slightly.

Batman felt the plant pod yield a tiny bit and he twisted his body towards the opening. He rolled over, shouldering his way out and leaving his cape behind. With a final push, he broke free and dropped onto the ground.

As soon as Batman was free, Robin let the trap snap shut again.

SNAP!

The Dark Knight stood up. He'd lost his cape but otherwise he looked completely unharmed.

Robin stared at Batman in disbelief. The Dark Knight had been soaking in digestive juices for so long! The Boy Wonder's own skin was still red from his swim in the monster plant. And his suit was sliced to ribbons by the constricting vine. But Batman looked . . . fine.

"My cape worked as a protective layer. It shielded me from the plant acids," Batman explained, noting Robin's surprise.

"It also kept me from getting caught in the hairs which are laced with potent nerve toxins to paralyse the plant's prey."

"At least we're both free." Robin sighed.

"True," the Caped Crusader replied. "But so is Poison Ivy."

CHAPTER 5

BELL JAR

It was dark under the dense canopy of leaves in Robinson Park. Robin stood rigid, afraid to touch anything growing around him. It seemed like every time he touched a plant something terrible happened.

Fighting Poison Ivy here, on her own turf with her army of vegetation, seemed impossible. Batman and Robin needed to lure her out of the park if they wanted to have any hope of capturing her. And they were running out of daylight.

Robin's partner stood nearby. Batman had been silent, lost in thought for some time. The Boy Wonder knew better than to interrupt his mentor when he was puzzling out a problem, but the fading light was making Robin nervous. The only thing worse than being stuck in Poison Ivy's nasty jungle would be being stuck here in the dark!

FWHOP! FWHOP! FWHOP! FWHOP!

The chopping sound of helicopter rotors roared overhead. Robin looked up, but he could not see anything through the dense overgrowth. Here and there a light glinted off of leaves, but the plant cover was so thick that the beam rarely reached the jungle floor.

Batman was looking up too.

Robin could not tell if the helicopter belonged to the police or not. He hoped it was somebody coming to help.

"Who's flying that thing?" the Boy Wonder asked.

"I am," Batman answered.

Robin had not noticed the tiny remote control device in Batman's hand. He wondered how Batman could fly the craft without being able to see it.

"How – ?" Robin started to ask.

"I've got an onscreen display," Batman explained, tapping his cowl. "I'm using cameras to see."

Robin nodded. The Dark Knight was full of surprises!

The sound of the rotors grew louder and Robin scanned overhead. He was looking for a ladder, or rope or line. He was anxious to get out of Poison Ivy's lair, and any escape route would do! But nothing appeared.

Instead, Batman started to move through the jungle on foot.

"Stay close, Robin," Batman instructed him. "I've found a clearing."

By using the cameras on the helicopter Batman had found a spot in the centre of the park that was not completely overgrown. And it looked like it was just large enough for what he had in mind.

Robin was careful not to touch any of the shrubbery around him as he followed the Dark Knight. He stepped only in Batman's footsteps. It was slow going, but at last the two of them made it to the clearing.

Robin looked up. Now that it was clear overhead the helicopter should be able to send down an escape line! But the lights on the helicopter were so bright Robin could not see a thing. And still no rope appeared.

"What are we waiting for? Let's get out of here!" Robin yelled over the noise.

"Not without Poison Ivy," Batman said. "Operation Glass House is about to begin!"

The Dark Knight leaned close to Robin and told him the plan. Robin thought it sounded like a long shot – but he trusted his partner completely. And it was their only hope of removing the most dangerous plant from the city park.

**

The helicopter continued to thunder overhead. Along with the noise, the spinning rotors also created whipping winds. Robin held his hand over his eyes and dropped to his knees on the edge of the clearing. Then the Boy Wonder began to pull fistfuls of plants out of the soil with his gloved hands.

He grabbed plants by the handful and tore them out by their roots. Throwing them aside, he went back for more.

"Nothing but weeds!" Robin shouted as he worked.

The boy thought hard about the awful vines he'd been trapped in earlier. He also thought about the thorns that had pricked him in the conservatory and the terrible pool in the slippery plant. Normally he liked plants. But this plant pulling project was all part of Batman's plan . . . and he had a strong feeling it would draw Poison Ivy out.

Sure enough, Poison Ivy suddenly appeared in the clearing!

"What are you *DOING*?" she screamed at Robin. "I thought I'd dealt with you meddlers! Why are you loose and destroying my garden?"

Robin didn't answer. He paused and let the clumps of uprooted plants fall from his fingers.

Poison Ivy was livid. Her eyes flashed.

Robin did not move. "I'm pulling *weeds*," he said, yanking out another handful.

Poison Ivy stamped her foot and clenched her hands into fists. Several seedlings sprouted spontaneously where her boot hit the soil. Making Poison Ivy even angrier was all part of Batman's plan.

"What did you call my precious plants?" Poison Ivy demanded. "Weeds?" She could not stand that term. "A weed is something that grows where it is not wanted. I think *you're* the weed here!"

Poison Ivy moved closer to Robin. Her fury was making her crazy.

Still Robin stayed where he was, crouched low to the ground. He could not look away from Poison Ivy. She wasn't thinking clearly, and he didn't know what she might do next. She looked like she wanted to give him the rash of a lifetime!

Out of the corner of his eye the Boy Wonder searched for Batman. He silently prayed that this plan would work.

Poison Ivy's eyes blazed. She reached both hands towards Robin's neck –

And at that moment Robin saw a bright flash across the clearing. It was the signal he had been waiting for!

Robin pushed a button on his Utility Belt. Instantly he was yanked away from Poison Ivy and pulled like a shot across the expanse of the clearing.

Blinded by rage, Poison Ivy did not stop to think. She ran after Robin! She reached the centre of the clearing with the noise of the helicopter pounding in her ears.

FWHOP! FWHOP! FWHOP! FWHOP!

Standing on the other side of the clearing Batman triggered the release of a giant dome that was hanging beneath the helicopter. His timing was perfect. The clear cage dropped down right on top of Poison Ivy. The green villain was trapped!

Batman stepped out of the shadows and pushed a few more buttons on his Batcopter's remote control. He tapped the hard wall of the super-strong polymer cage. The see-through enclosure was a recent invention he'd designed with Alfred in the Batcave. It hadn't been tested but seemed to be working well.

Poison Ivy pounded on the other side of the rigid material. "You can't keep me in here!" she screamed. She stomped her feet on the floor. She wanted to summon her seedling armies. She wanted to activate her killer spores. But nothing happened.

"We've made you a private greenhouse, Ivy," Batman said. "And we've cut off access to all of your little friends."

Poison Ivy dropped to her knees. She pounded the ground. It was covered with a layer of the same polymer the dome was made of. It was sterile and nearly unbreakable.

While Robin was distracting Poison Ivy by uprooting plants, Batman had spread a synthetic floor out in the clearing. The high-tech plastic sealed itself to the bottom of the bell jar upon contact.

The floor of Ivy's greenhouse prison made a barrier between her and all of the other living plant organisms in her jungle. She could not call on her plant army or the millions of microbes in the soil. She was sealed up tight.

Batman pushed the retract button on his remote control. The clear dome began to lift off the ground, taking Poison Ivy with it. She continued to yell at her captors as she was carried up and away.

Robin opened his mouth to speak, but Batman put up his finger. "Just a moment, Robin. I need to make a phone call. I have to let Arkham Asylum know they have a returning guest on the way. As soon as she's been dropped off I'll bring the Batcopter back to pick us up."

Relief flooded Robin's body. He was happy to see Ivy go and happier to know he would be heading home soon too.

"It looks like you got to the root of that problem," Robin joked when Batman had finished his call.

Batman didn't laugh. He didn't even smile. He knew there was a method to Poison Ivy's madness. Protecting plants wasn't a bad thing. But Ivy took it too far. He also knew that Poison Ivy would be back. The plant part of her had an amazing will to survive, even against horrible odds. The Queen of Green had unstoppable determination. It reminded Batman of the way dandelions sometimes grew in the cracks of the pavement. Poison Ivy would definitely be back, and probably when she was least expected.

POISON IVY

REAL NAME: Pamela Isley

OCCUPATION: Professional criminal, botanist

BASE: Gotham City

HEIGHT: 1.7 metres [5 feet 6 inches]

WEIGHT: 50 kilograms [110 pounds]

EYES: Green

HAIR: Red

Born with immunities to plant toxins and poisons, Pamela Isley's love of plants began to grow like a weed at an early age. She eventually became a botanist. Through reckless experimentation with various flora, Pamela Isley's skin itself has become poisonous. Her venomous lips and poisonous plant weapons present a real problem for the Dynamic Duo. But Ivy's most dangerous quality is her extreme love of nature – she cares more about the smallest seed than any human life.

- Poison Ivy was once engaged to Gotham City's District Attorney, Harvey Dent, who eventually became the super-villain Two-Face! Their relationship ended when Dent built a prison on a field of wildflowers, unintentionally provoking Ivy's wrath.

- Poison Ivy emits toxic fragrances that can be harmful to humans. Whenever she is locked up in Arkham Asylum, a wall of perspex must separate her from the guards to ensure their safety.

- Ivy's connection to plants is so strong that she can control them by thought alone! The control she has over her lethal plants makes her a dangerous foe for Gotham City Police – as well as Batman and Robin.

BIOGRAPHIES

Sarah Hines Stephens has been a children's book reader, editor, seller, buyer, author, copyeditor and ghostwriter for nearly 20 years – and she is still most of those things. She has published more than 100 books for children both original and licenced, and written about characters including Jedi, curious monkeys, super heroes, powerful princesses and disgruntled fowl. She lives in California, USA, with her husband, two children and two dogs. When she is not doing book-related things, Sarah enjoys cooking, gardening, travelling, spending time with friends and family and dancing around in her kitchen.

Tim Levins is best known for his work on the Eisner Award-winning DC Comics series Batman: Gotham Adventures. Tim has illustrated other DC titles, such as Justice League Adventures, Batgirl, Metal Men and Scooby Doo, and has also done work for Marvel Comics and Archie Comics. Tim enjoys life in Ontario, Canada, with his wife, son and two dogs.

GLOSSARY

bonsai miniature tree or shrub, grown in a pot for decoration

botanist biologist specializing in the study of plants

carnivourous eating meat

chaperone adult who protects the safety of young people at an event and who makes sure they behave well

chlorophyll chemical that plants use to capture the energy in sunlight

conservatory greenhouse used for grown plants

enzyme substance that helps break down food

instinct behaviour that is natural rather than learned

restoration bringing something back to its original condition

rotor set of rotating blades that lifts an aircraft off of the ground

sterile free of germs and dirt

DISCUSSION QUESTIONS

1. Alfred says that sometimes plants need to be pruned so that everyone can enjoy them. Do you think Poison Ivy would agree with Bruce Wayne's butler? Discuss why you think she would or wouldn't agree with him.

2. Why does Poison Ivy take over Robinson Park? What does she hope to accomplish? List your ideas and discuss her most likely motives.

3. Batman and Robin capture Poison Ivy in a large bell jar. Why do you think their trap worked? What are some other ways they could have captured her instead? Explain your answers.

WRITING PROMPTS

1. Batman and Robin use a variety of gadgets and tools from their Utility Belts to escape Poison Ivy's plants. If you had a Utility Belt, what tools would you carry in it? Make a list, then describe the one you think would work best on Poison Ivy's villainous plants.

2. Poison Ivy controls plants to commit her crimes and battle the Dynamic Duo. Find a plant in your house, at school or outside, and describe what it looks like. Then make a list of things your plant could do if Poison Ivy controlled it.

3. Batman and Robin use a clever trap to capture Poison Ivy. Write a short story where the Dynamic Duo must use a complicated trap to capture Two-Face, the Joker or some other super-villain.

DC

BATMAN & ROBIN ADVENTURES